**AUTUMN**
PUBLISHING

*Published in 2020*
*First published in the UK by Igloo Books Ltd*
*An imprint of Igloo Books Ltd*
*Cottage Farm, NN6 0BJ, UK*
*Owned by Bonnier Books*
*Sveavägen 56, Stockholm, Sweden*
*www.igloobooks.com*



1020 004
4 6 8 10 9 7 5 3
ISBN 978-1-83903-038-3

Illustrated by David Creighton-Pester
Written by Melanie Joyce

Cover designed by Nicholas Gage and Lee Italiano
Interiors designed by Lee Italiano

Edited by Helen Catt

Printed and manufactured in China

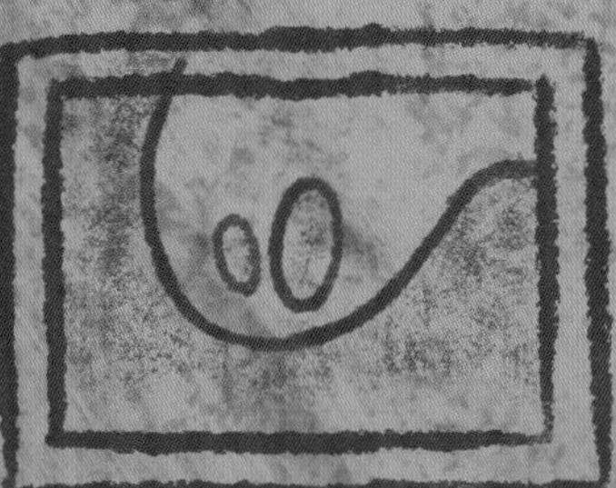

The
BEAR
ON
THE
STAIR
AUTUMN
PUBLISHING

Once, I saw a

BEAR.

It was right there,
on the
STAIR.

It wasn't a scary bear.

It had **crazy** hair,

and did **jumping jacks** in the **air**.

Mom said, "There's nothing there."

But I didn't care.
I saw that
bear.

"Hey there," said the bear.

Then he ran up the stair.

I followed him up the stair...

...and guess what was there?

An elephant was sitting on a chair,
trumpeting tunes to a tap-dancing hare,
DANCE

while two tall flamingoes twirled in a pair,

and a hippo in a top hat ate an éclair.

"ROAR!"

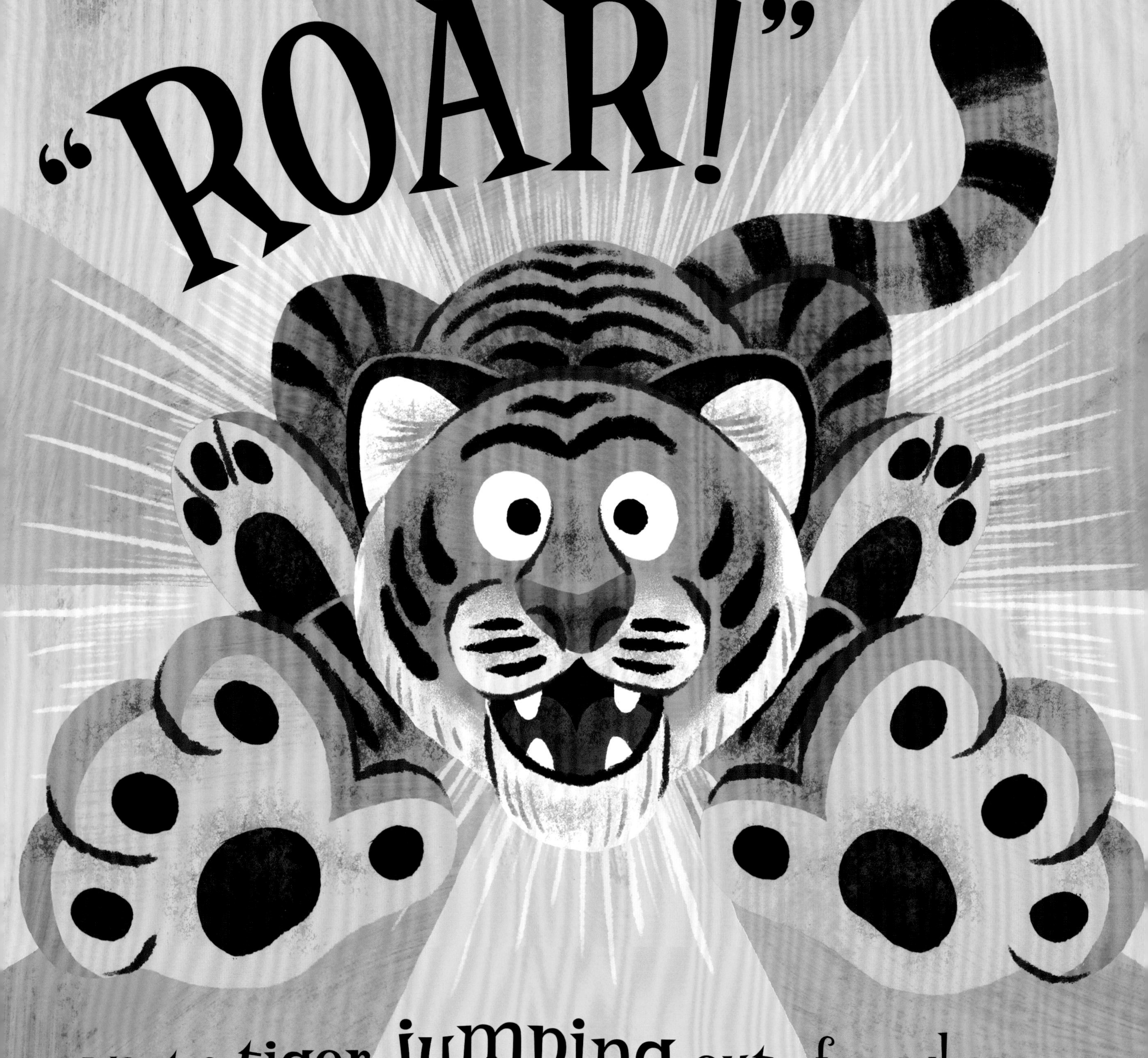

went a tiger, **jumping** out of nowhere . . .

... making the elephant fall off his chair.

He just wanted to play, but he gave me a scare.

"Let's have a party,"
declared the bear.

"Hop to it!" cried the hare to everyone there,
even the tiger who gave me a scare.

What a party we had, at the top of the stair.

There were silly games . . .

. . . and cakes to share (with lots to spare). . .
. . . and mess everywhere.

Then I heard a **creak** somewhere on the **stair**.

"Go and look," said the bear.

So I crept down the stair,

and **guess who** was there?

It was Mom with my teddy bear.

"Time for bed," she said.

"No more playing up there."

"Goodnight,"

I whispered to the bear on the stair.